Way Down Deep
in the
Deep Blue Sea

by
Jan Peck

illustrated by
Valeria Petrone

POCKET BOOKS
London New York Sydney

My deepest heartfelt thanks to David R. Davis, Cerelle Woods, Melissa Russell, Kathryn Lay, Diane Roberts, BJ Stone, Janet Fick, Debra Deur, Chris Ford, Tom McDermott, Sue Ward, Deborah J. Lightfoot, Trish Holland, Amanda Jenkins, and my editor, Kevin L. Lewis—J. P.

POCKET
BOOKS

This edition published in 2004 by Pocket Books,
an imprint of Simon & Schuster UK Ltd
Africa House, 64-78 Kingsway, London WC2B 6AH

Originally published in 2004 by Simon & Schuster Books for Young Readers,
an imprint of Simon & Schuster Children's Publishing Division, New York

Book designed by Gregory Stadnyk
The text for this book is set in Fink Heavy
The illustrations are rendered digitally

A CIP catalogue record for this book is available from the British Library upon request

ISBN 0-743-48984-5
Manufactured in China
1 3 5 7 9 10 8 6 4 2

first
edition

To my Four Star Critique Group,
and my editor, Kevin L. Lewis—J. P.

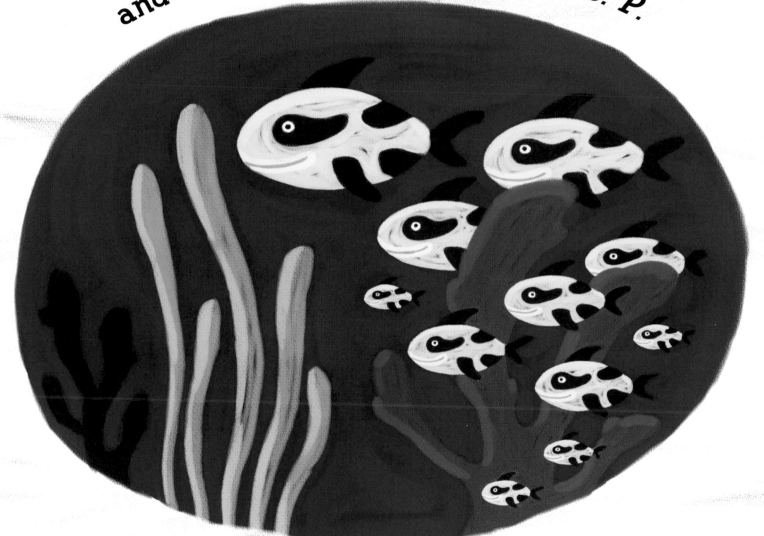

For Rosie and Phoebe—V. P.

Way down deep in the deep blue sea,
I'm looking for a treasure
for my mummy and me.
I'm so brave,
can't scare me,
way down deep in the deep blue sea.

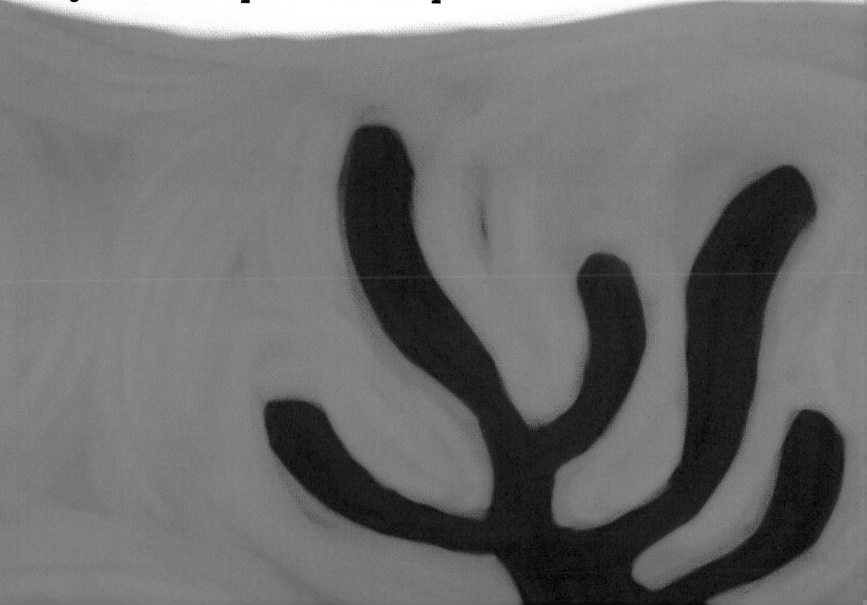

Way down deep in the deep blue sea,
I spy a sea horse racing by me.
Hello, sea horse.
Giddy-up, sea horse.
See you later, sea horse.

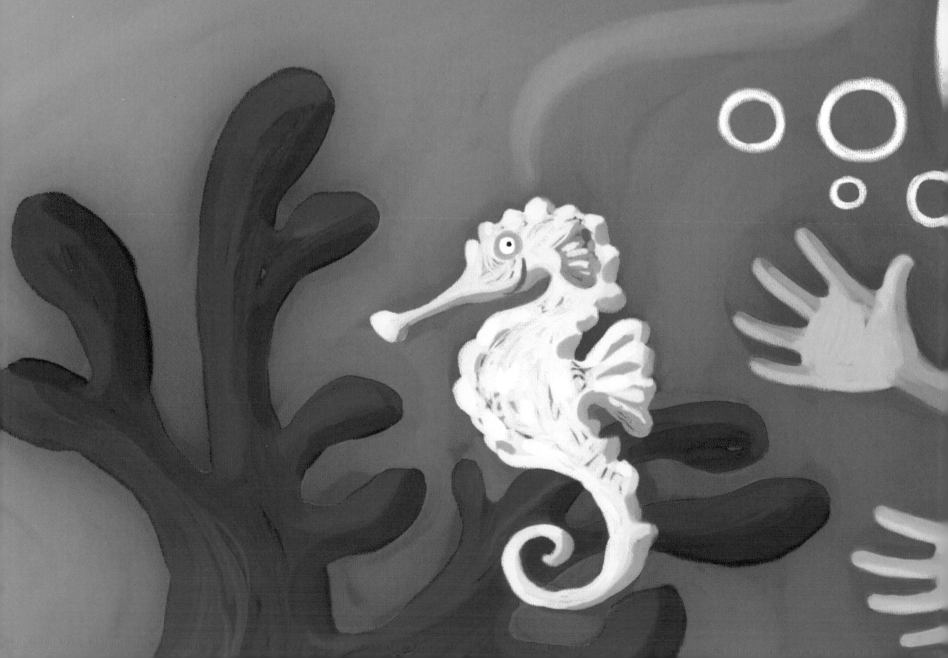

Swim away.

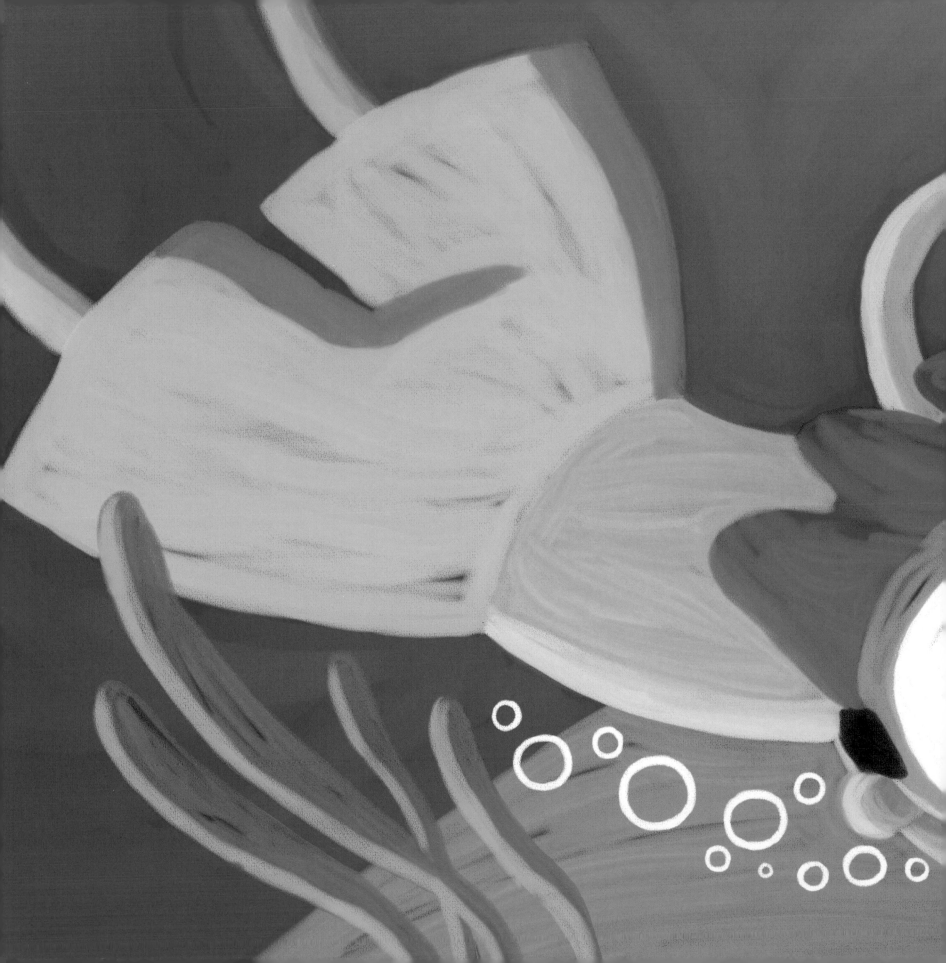

Way down deep in the deep blue sea,
I spy a hermit crab hiding from me.
Hello, crab.
Peek-a-boo, crab.
See you later, crab.

Swim away.

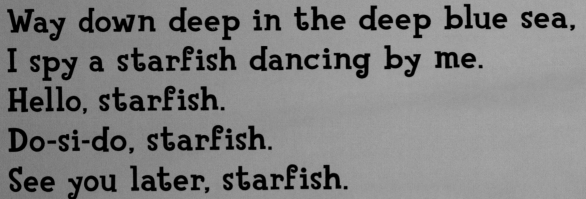

Way down deep in the deep blue sea,
I spy a starfish dancing by me.
Hello, starfish.
Do-si-do, starfish.
See you later, starfish.

Swim away.

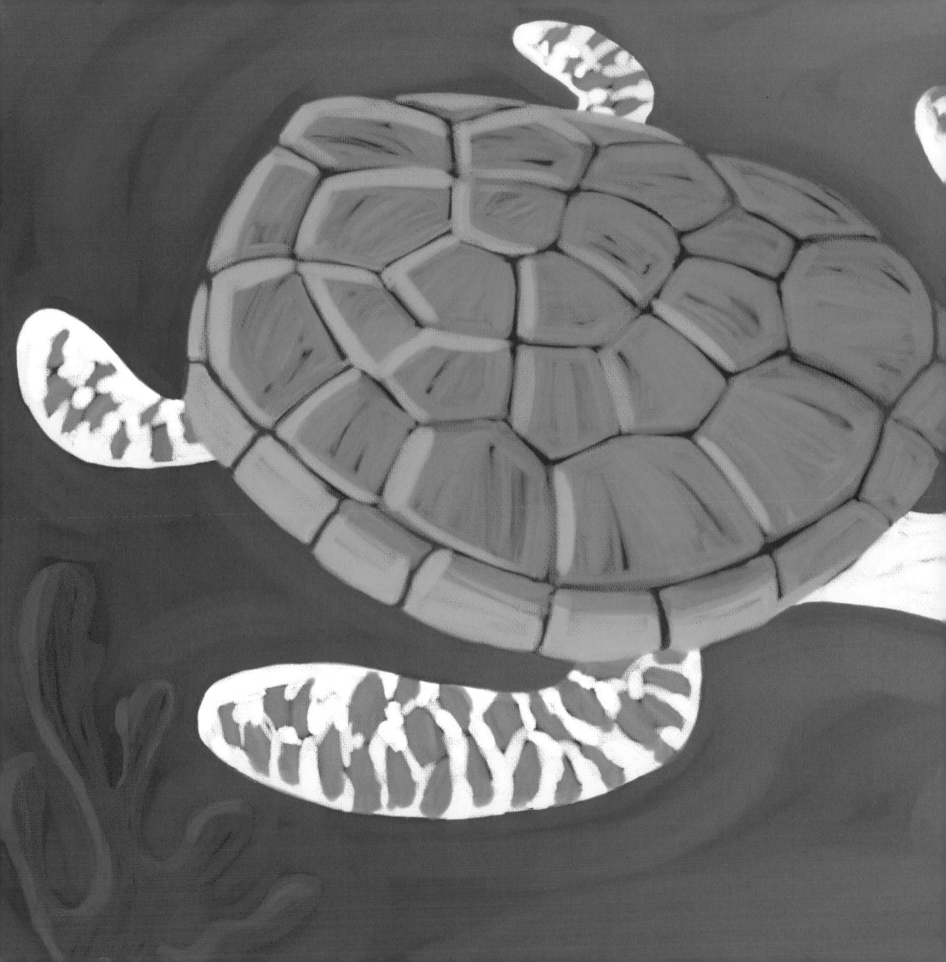

Way down deep in the deep blue sea,
I spy a sea turtle following me.
Hello, turtle.
Tag along, turtle.
See you later, turtle.

Swim away.

Way down deep in the deep blue sea,
I spy an octopus waving at me.
Hello, octopus.
Gimme eight, octopus.
See you later, octopus.

Swim away.

Way down deep in the deep blue sea,
I spy a dolphin diving by me.
Hello, dolphin.
Hitch a ride, dolphin.
See you later, dolphin.

Swim away.

Way down deep in the deep blue sea,
I spy a swordfish fencing with me.
Hello, swordfish.
Touché, swordfish.
See you later, swordfish.

Swim away.

Way down deep in the deep blue sea,
I spy a whale spouting water by me.
Hello, whale.
Sing along, whale.
See you later, whale.

Swim away.

Way down deep in the deep blue sea,
I spy treasure gleaming at me.
Hello, treasure.
Pirate treasure.
Take-along treasure.

Swim away.

Way down deep in the deep blue sea,
I spy a shark laughing at me!

Good-bye, shark!

Good-bye, whale!
Good-bye, swordfish!
Good-bye, dolphin!

Good-bye, octopus!
Good-bye, turtle!
Good-bye, starfish!
Good-bye, hermit crab!
Good-bye, sea horse!

Up, up, up from the deep blue sea,
I find Mummy waiting for me.
Hello, Mummy!
Guess what, Mummy?
I found treasure in the deep blue sea!

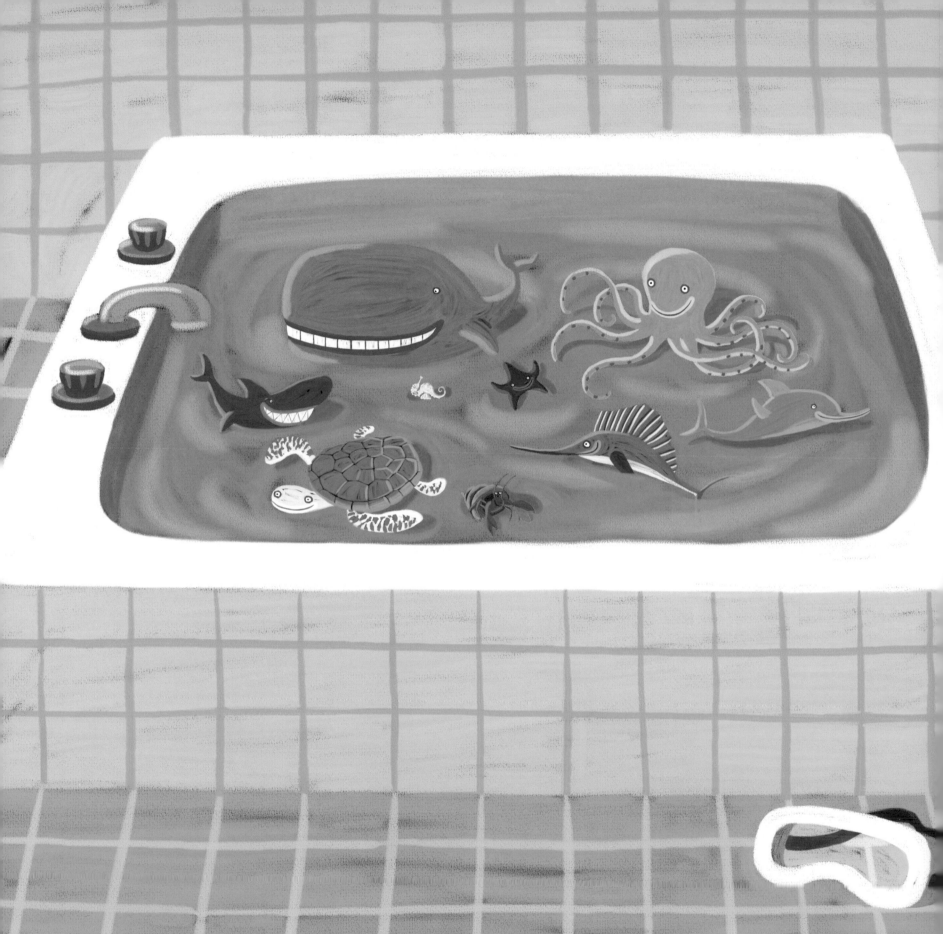